SYTHID THE SPIDER CRAB

BY ADAM BLADE

N
W
E
S
THE LOST CAVES OF CHI
THE STONE BREASTPLATE
THE PEARL SPEAR
THE ROCKY ISLAND
STILLFISH SHOALS

> OCEANS OF NEMOS: THE CHAOS QUADRANT
THE CORAL SWORD
THE PORT OF BARRIOSA
THE SHELL HELMET
THE GRAVE OF THE CORAL GIANTS

I have waited in the shadows long enough, perfecting myself. Now I will strike at my wretched enemies and make all Nemos bow before me. All I need to complete my plan are the Arms of Addulis: the Spear, the Breastplate, the Sword and the Helmet.

My mother used to tell me stories of their power, and for a long time I thought they were myths. But now I know they are real, buried in this vast ocean and waiting for a new master to wield them. With the Arms of Addulis in my control, no Merryn or human will be able to stop me.

But… I almost hope there is some pathetic hero foolish enough to try. My Robobeasts are ready – unlike anything these oceans have witnessed before. My enemies will learn that their flesh is weak.

Quake before your new leader!

RED EYE

CHAPTER ONE

UNEXPECTED GUESTS

"Ten points!" yelled Max as his aquabowl disc struck the final floating pin and sent it bobbing across the surface of the pool.

The secluded bowling pool lay in a corner of Aquora's harbour, in the shade of the great city's silver towers and needle-sharp skyscrapers. It was surrounded by banks of seating for spectators, although they were mostly empty today. Strings of coloured lights hung everywhere, and a band was

playing, adding to the festive atmosphere.

"It's a stupid game," grumbled Lia, picking up another disc, a smooth plate of white metal that flashed with blue and amber lights. So far, Lia hadn't managed to hit a single target. Using technology didn't come naturally to her – even something as simple as an aquabowl disc.

"It's fun once you've had a bit of practice," Max promised, as he pressed a button to set the targets up again.

"Fine – watch this!" declared Lia, a crafty expression coming over her face as she dived into the pool. She pulled her Amphibio mask off and let out a series of high calls.

Moments later, a shoal of blue flying fish appeared, leaping from the harbour and plunging into the pool.

Max watched as Lia used her amazing Aqua Powers to command the shoal. *That's cheating*, he thought, as one by one, the leaping fish knocked down the targets.

"*That's* how to play aquabowl!" Lia said with a grin.

"Fine, you win," Max accepted grudgingly. "But that's not really in the rules!"

It felt good to be relaxing, with the danger of their recent adventures behind them. It wasn't long since Max and Lia had defeated the Robobeast Drakkos created by his wicked uncle, the Professor. Now the Professor was safely locked up – and his associate, the terrifying pirate Cora Blackheart, was marooned in the Lost Lagoon. Life was peaceful in Aquora these days. Rivet, Max's faithful dogbot, was off somewhere in the harbour with Lia's swordfish, Spike, teaching each other their favourite underwater tricks.

Lia sprang from the pool, the Amphibio mask back over her nose and mouth, giving her the precious oxygen that all Merryn people needed to survive above water.

"Now what shall we do?" she asked. "No more silly games. Something *interesting*."

"I know what you mean," Max replied. It was great to be out of danger, but he was itching for a little bit more excitement.

As if in answer to his thoughts, his wrist

communicator flashed and his mother's smiling face appeared on the screen.

"Max, someone's come to visit you," she told him. "He's waiting for you in the apartment."

"Who?" Max asked.

"You'll see." Her face vanished.

"Come on," said Lia. "I've had enough of thrashing you at aquabowl!"

They made their way through the busy streets of Aquora, the shining towers and tapering skyscrapers of the city rising up around them. Transport vehicles hovered in the air, and here and there, people gathered in clusters under huge Holonews billboards, watching the latest reports from the Aquoran High Council. Max recognised some of the important City Councillors he and Lia had met after their last Quest, when they had been celebrated as heroes of Aquora.

Soon they came to the multi-storey apartment block where Max and his parents lived. It was the tallest building in the city, and Max lived very near the top. They crossed the high-ceilinged entrance lobby and stepped into one of the glass elevators. Max touched a pressure pad and the elevator shot upwards, carrying them in moments to the five hundred and twenty-third floor.

Getting out, they walked down the corridor to Max's home. Max tapped in the entry code and the door slid open, and they made their way into the sleek white, ultra-high-tech apartment with its touch screens and motion sensors.

Max let out a cry of pleasure when he saw their old friend Roger, seated at his ease and drinking tea with Max's parents, Callum and Niobe.

Roger jumped up, his long grey ponytail

bouncing, his craggy face creased into a wide smile.

"Well, if it ain't me old messmates Max and Lia!" he roared. As he strode forwards, his hook hand hit a vase and sent it tumbling. Max noticed his dad wince as the vase shattered on the floor.

"Sorry, mateys," mumbled Roger, holding up the glittering hook. "I should be used to it by now, but I keep forgetting!" He shook his head. "My memory's not what it was, I fear."

"Don't worry about it, Roger," said Niobe, with a wave of her hand. Callum looked like he was going to say something, then thought better of it. Max had a soft spot for Roger but he could understand why Aquora's Chief Defence Engineer might feel a little hostile to their pirate guest.

"I suppose a man like you needs the open sea," said Max, as he collected up the broken shards of the vase and put them down the recycling chute. "I wasn't expecting to see you here in Aquora!"

"It's true, the life of a landlubber ain't for me," Roger declared, his one good eye twinkling. He gestured to the window. "Take a look, my new ship is at anchor in the docks."

Everyone gathered round, and Roger handed Max a pair of powerful binoculars. He looked out of the window and saw the ship Roger pointed out by the quay. It was sleek and shining, and bore the skull and crossbones.

"It's impressive," Callum admitted.

"Very," added Niobe. "Roger's done well for himself."

"She's called the *Lizard's Revenge*," said Roger, proudly.

Lia frowned at him. "Did you steal it?"

Roger's face split into a wide grin. "Good gracious, no! I *liberated* her. She has a hold full of booty – and booty belongs to whoever finds it. That's the age-old Pirate Code."

Max saw his father's eyes narrow, and Niobe laid a calming hand on his arm in reassurance.

"Will you take us to look over it?" Max

asked Roger hastily.

"Of course!" said Roger.

A small voice piped up from behind Max. "That's not fair! You promised to show me Aquora first!" Max turned. A small girl of about six years old had just come out of the bathroom, and was staring at them with a deep frown. She was dressed like an old-fashioned pirate in a yellow silk blouse and purple trousers tucked into tall brown leather boots.

"Ah yes," said Niobe. "I nearly forgot… Max and Lia, this is Grace. She's Roger's niece."

"What about my tour?" said Grace, insistently.

"I did promise you a tour of Aquora, and that's the honest truth of it," admitted Roger. "Come here, Grace, and say hello to my friends." The girl stepped forwards, staring

at Max and Lia with one bright blue eye – the other hidden behind an eye patch just like her uncle's.

"Hello, Grace," said Max, stepping forward to shake her hand.

Grace pulled a toy blaster from her belt. "Keep back!" she growled fiercely.

Startled, Max backed off.

"I like her!" said Lia with a laugh. "She's feisty."

"She doesn't really need the eye patch," Roger confided. "But she's a pirate through and through! I couldn't ask for a better shipmate."

"We'll show you around Aquora," said Lia. "We can look at the ship afterwards."

Max's dad rose and took Max by the arm. "Can we trust him?" he muttered, low enough that Roger couldn't hear.

"Of course, Dad," Max replied. "After all, this is Aquora. If we're not safe here –"

His words were cut off by something shrieking through the sky outside, its high-pitched whine audible through the glass panes of the windows.

"Look!" shouted Max, his heart racing as he pointed to a slender trail of white smoke that curved down from the sky and struck a building by the docks. There was a bloom of red flame and a massive explosion.

"It's a missile!" cried Max's father.

Aquora is under attack!

CHAPTER TWO

SHOCK ATTACK

"You go, Callum," said Niobe, ushering him to the door. "I'll stay here and make sure the building is evacuated."

Callum nodded and led the others as they raced out of the apartment and into the elevator. "It must be a raid," muttered Max's father. He glared at Roger, who was helping Grace and Lia into the elevator. "Pirates, perhaps?"

The pirate shook his head. "I had nothing to do with this, I swear!" he said.

"Pirates are noble and honourable!" piped Grace, scowling at Max's father.

The elevator reached the ground floor and they raced through the lobby and out into the streets. They were filled with people, running wildly in every direction.

Callum jabbed at his wrist control and spoke into it. "This is Chief Defence Engineer North speaking," he said. "I'm heading for the site of the attack. Can you tell me why our long-range sensors didn't pick up the missile or the vessel that launched it?"

"We're looking into it, sir," came the reply.

"Perhaps the attackers have sensor-blocking technology?" Max suggested. *Even the Professor never had that kind of advanced weaponry.*

A disturbing idea struck him. *Do we have a new enemy?*

"Keep me informed," ordered Max's father,

running towards the building that had been hit – a defensive fort next to the docks.

Max followed. He soon saw that there was a black hole punched into the building's side, and debris was scattered across the streets. A few people were helping the injured away while flames flickered above.

"Look!" gasped Lia, pointing out to the harbour. Two huge, sleek submarines had surfaced – one on either side of Roger's ship.

Max stared at the vessels. Their hulls were made of a strange blue-grey metal, and bristled with guns. Emblazoned on the prow of each of the subs was a skull and crossbones. But the skulls had piercing red eyes.

So they are *pirates*, thought Max.

Attackers were swarming out of the subs,

boarding Roger's ship. Others had jumped onto the docks, holding off the harbour guards with high-powered blaster rifles.

"They're trying to steal my ship!" cried Roger.

Max blinked at the pirates. Something about them wasn't right. "I don't think they're…human," Max said. "They're like metal skeletons."

"And look at their strange glowing red

eyes!" added Lia, agreeing.

They're robots! Max realised, with a lurch of his stomach.

The cybernetic pirates had long, thin limbs like metal bones, and wore black tunics emblazoned with a huge red eye.

One of them spotted Max and his companions and delivered a blast of fire that made them duck for cover behind a stack of crates.

"I'm not scared of them!" declared Grace, though she was pale and trembling.

"I know these scoundrels!" Roger said, fearfully. "They're called cyrates."

"Who's controlling them?" asked Max.

"A vicious new pirate king who calls himself Red Eye," said Roger. " He's taken over the Chaos Quadrant."

Max's heart sank. He had heard of that part of Nemos – it was a barbarous and violent region where the very worst pirates lived.

"Leave my uncle's ship alone, you stupid cyrates!" yelled Grace, jumping up and brandishing her plastic blaster at the robotic pirates. They were already pressing the harbour guards back as they advanced along the jetties.

"Get down!" cried Lia, pulling Grace back under cover as a blast struck the top of the crate where she had been standing.

Callum spoke into his wrist communicator. "I need reinforcements at the southern docks, pier 243."

Suddenly Max had an idea. "Dad? Will you and your Defence Officers keep the cyrates busy while we board the ship?'

Max's dad gave him a long look. At last he nodded. "But be careful." He raced across the docks to join the other Defence Officers.

Max slipped a headset on and spoke into

the mic. "Max to Rivet – come, boy!'

An electronic voice crackled in his ear. "Coming, Max!"

"Ready?" Max asked Lia. She nodded. The two of them sped away along a jetty, leaving Roger hugging Grace tight, as she squirmed to break free and follow after them.

As soon as they reached the end, they dived off the jetty into the water. *I'm so glad I have the Merryn Touch*, Max thought, as they slipped underwater. He felt his gills beginning to work, drawing oxygen from the sea. They powered in the direction of Roger's sub, the undersides of Aquoran ships looming darkly around them.

At his side, Lia glided effortlessly through the water. Max watched as she touched the fingers of one hand to her forehead, her eyes narrowing in concentration.

A few seconds later, Lia's pet swordfish

Spike arrived, drawn to them by Lia's Aqua Powers.

"Spike will keep watch for us," Lia told Max.

Another shape came speeding towards them. It was Rivet, his red snout-lamp glowing brightly in the murky harbour water.

"Rivet here!" the dogbot declared.

"We have to get aboard Roger's ship, boy," said Max, pointing to the surface, where flashes of blaster fire lit up the *Lizard's Revenge*.

They swam upwards, emerging in the gap between the hull of Roger's ship and the side of one of the two submarines flanking it. Max glanced around anxiously, half-expecting to feel the heat of a cyrate's blaster ray at any moment.

"Rivet, engage magnets," Max said. The

dogbot clamped his humming feet to the side of the sub and scuttled swiftly up the hull while Max and Lia clambered behind. They stopped with the gunwale just above them. Max's heart was hammering in his chest as he peered over the edge, but the deck was deserted. *The cyrates must be below – maybe searching for something*, Max thought. *What has Roger stolen this time?*

"Stay here, boy," he whispered to Rivet. "Let me know if we're spotted."

"Max be careful," said the dogbot over the crackle and boom of the fire fight on the docks.

Max and Lia crept quickly along the deck, frantically looking for a way up onto the bridge. They were halfway up a staircase when Max heard a hissing sound and blaster fire struck the rail close to his hand.

A near miss!

He spun around and saw a cyrate down on the deck behind them, aiming for another shot. Max pulled his hyperblade from his belt, the vernium metal ringing in the air. He launched himself off the stairs and crashed down on the cyrate. A single blow sent the robot's skull-like head spinning from its

shoulders, and the spindly body collapsed on the deck.

Up close, the cyrate looked even more terrifying. Its bone-like metal fingers twitched as the red lights died in its wide dark sockets.

Max pulled the deactivated cyrate's blaster from its fingers and headed back up the stairs to where Lia was waiting. They sprinted towards the bridge. Out of nowhere, several cyrates barred their path and they were forced to dive for cover as the deadly robots fired on them.

"Down here!" gasped Max, pulling open a hatch for Lia to jump into. Dropping down after her, he felt the searing heat of blaster fire just over his head. With hands shaking from adrenaline, he sealed the hatch behind him.

Now they were below deck, Max saw

immediately that this was not like the sleek, shiny ships of the Aquoran fleet – more like an old-fashioned pirate vessel, with a ragged charm. Circular portholes gave the interior a dingy light, and there were hammocks and wooden furnishings. There was a strong smell of brine, and littering the floor were chests full of plunder, overflowing with gold and silver tableware, exotic coins and bright jewels.

Max turned to Lia. “Why aren’t they trying to take this away?”

“Perhaps they’re not looking for treasure,” Lia said.

So what are they looking for?

Suddenly the ship vibrated under their feet.

“That’s the sound of engines revving up,” said Max. “But not this ship’s engines. The submarines must be getting ready to leave!”

"Why would they do that?" asked Lia.

"Maybe because they've already got what they came here for!" shouted Max, running up a ramp towards the deck. "Whatever it is...we have to stop them!"

As he charged outside, Max's heart fell. The last of the cyrates was standing at the open hatch of the nearest submarine, watching

them with robotic coldness. A grating voice cut through the air.

"Tell Roger that Red Eye sends his regards," it said. "We'll be back soon enough...to destroy Aquora once and for all!"

The metal creature dropped through the hatch.

Max watched helplessly as the submarines turned and raced away from Aquora at incredible speed, sinking beneath the waves as they went.

The cyrates had escaped. And judging by those triumphant words, Max had a bad feeling they had got what they came for.

CHAPTER THREE

THE SEAWEED MAP

Roger and Grace came running up the gangplank. Grace was still gripping her toy blaster with a ferocious look in her eye, but Roger seemed panic-stricken. "Is my treasure gone?"

"I don't think they touched it," said Max.

A relieved grin creased Roger's face. "You drove them off before they could rob me!" he said. "I'd have come sooner, but an old battle wound slowed me down."

"You said it was safer for us to stay behind the crates, Uncle," Grace piped up.

"I meant safer for you, my dear," Roger said quickly.

"But that's not what you said…" Grace began.

"Be quiet, there's a good girl," interrupted Roger, patting her head.

"Hmm," said Max, suppressing a smile. He inspected the cyrate's blaster, which he still held. It had three firing barrels, enhanced for high-powered and rapid fire.

Hearing voices, he turned and saw a group of Aquoran Defence Officers moving towards the ship.

His dad was among them, clutching his arm, and one of the guards was supporting him.

Oh no...Dad's injured!

"What's wrong?" Max called anxiously.

"Nothing," his dad replied. "A blaster caught me, that's all."

Max vaulted over the side of the ship and ran to his dad, heart pounding. The sleeve of Callum's tunic was scorched and there was blood staining it.

"We need to get you to a medic," Max said, looking into his dad's pale face.

"There's no need," his father insisted, but he grimaced as he spoke.

"Either we get a medic right now…" Max held up his arm with the wrist communicator – "or I call Mum and tell her that you're being stubborn."

A resigned look came over his father's face. "Very well," he said.

Max called to a man wearing the yellow uniform of an Aquoran Medical Officer, patrolling the harbour for wounded guards.

The medic raced over to Callum,

withdrawing a medi-scan device, which he immediately swept over the wound. A second later it projected a 3-D holographic X-ray, along with an assessment of tissue damage and blood levels.

"It was wise of you to call me over," said

the doctor. "This wound needs attention."

Max was too smart to say "told you so".

An elderly white-haired man strode over, accompanied by a small squadron of personal guards. It was Chief Councillor Glenon – the most powerful man in Aquora.

"How's my Chief Defence Engineer?" Glenon asked.

"No lasting damage," said the doctor. "The meds we'll give him will stop infection, but he'll need to rest for a few weeks."

"That's not possible, I'm afraid," said Max's father. "We must discover the purpose of the attack."

Lia stepped forward. "We think they took something from Roger's ship."

"You are Roger, I take it," said Councillor Glenon, casting a sidelong glance at the pirate, standing back from the crowd with Grace at his side. "So what did they take?"

"To tell the truth, I've no idea," admitted Roger, rubbing his chin. "I've only had the ship a few days. I had no time to examine the cargo."

"Rivet saw!" Max's dogbot barked suddenly. "Rivet recorded it."

He must have switched on his eye cameras, thought Max.

"Great work, Rivet!" Max pressed a small button on Rivet's snout which projected the camera recording. It showed cyrates leaping from Roger's ship onto the submarine and diving down the hatch.

"None of them have anything but blasters in their hands," said Lia.

"Wait," said Max, and his dogbot paused the playback on a freeze-frame. He stabbed a finger at the image. "What's that?"

One of the cyrates was carrying a large sheet under its arm.

"Zoom, Rivet," said Max. The frozen frame grew larger to give a clearer picture.

"It's a map!" Max exclaimed. "There's writing on it, and the outlines of an island, or something."

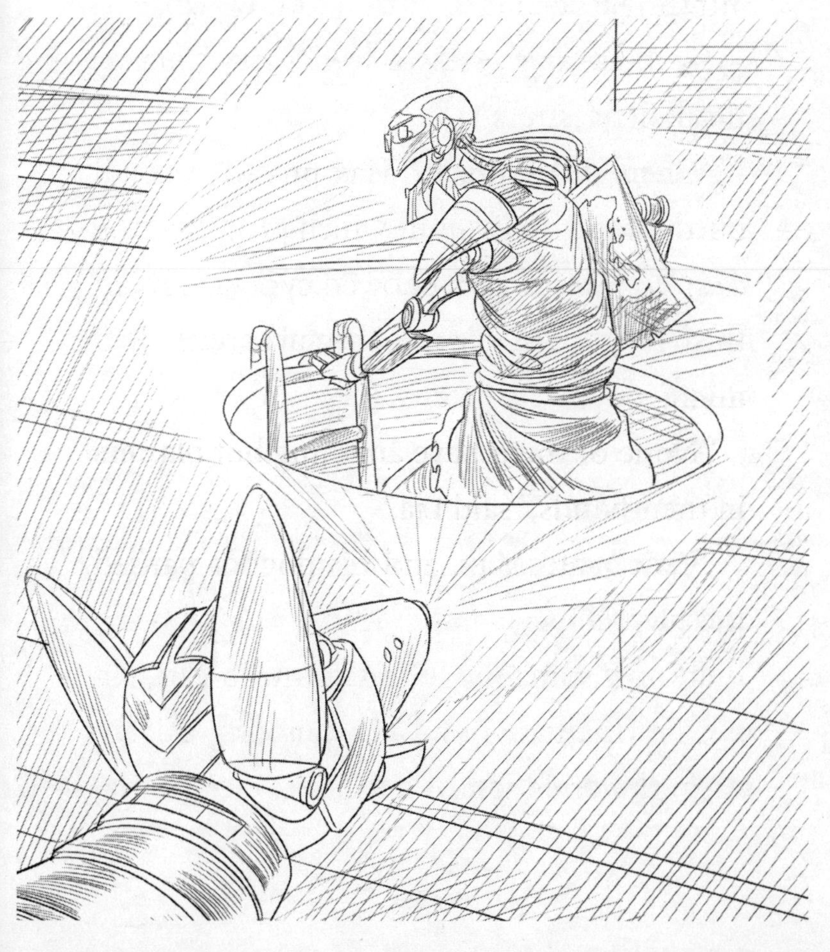

"What language is that?" asked Councillor Glenon, peering at the writing.

"It's old Merryn script," said Lia, examining the rune-like lettering. "Old documents like these were made from sheets of seaweed." She shook her head. "I don't know what it says – these days, only a few Merryn know the ancient letters."

"Where did you get this map?" Max's dad asked Roger.

"I've never seen it before," said Roger. "It must have been hidden somewhere in the hold."

"Are those Xs?" asked Max, pointing at the frozen image.

"X means treasure," murmured Roger, his eyes gleaming.

"I know someone in Sumara who can tell us what they are," said Lia, pointing out to sea in the direction of her home city. "Tarla the old healing woman."

"Lia and I will go to Sumara and ask her what it says," said Max, eagerly. "Once we know that, we should be able to work out what Red Eye wants with it."

"Hold on, young man," said Glenon. "It doesn't matter to us if this Red Eye is using robots to dig up some buried treasure. The important thing is that they've gone."

Max faced the Chief Councillor. "With respect sir, the cyrates threatened to come back. That means Aquora might still be in danger. We have to do this."

"Niobe will want to come with you," said Max's father.

Councillor Glenon cleared his throat. "I can't allow that," he said sternly. "With Callum injured, the city will need Niobe more than ever."

"I want to go!" Grace chimed in, staring up

at her uncle. "You promised me adventures, Uncle Roger!" She folded her arms and gave him a cross look. "And I'm fed up with being dragged around a lot of smelly old pirate taverns!"

"That's enough, Grace, dear," Roger cut in, his face glowing red with embarrassment. He smiled weakly at the others. "We'll go on my ship," he blustered, pointing to the *Lizard's Revenge*. "She's quicker than she looks, with top of the range cannons – and big enough for us all."

"Very well," said Councillor Glenon, eyeing Roger. "At least it will rid us of one pirate." He turned to Max and Lia. "We have engineers working on how those robots got past the sensors – I'll make sure they won't be a threat again. But go, if you must. You've proved yourself before."

"We won't let you down," said Max. "We'll

find out what Red Eye wants, and we'll stop him!"

Excitement surged through his body.

Another Sea Quest is about to begin!

CHAPTER FOUR

VOYAGE TO SUMARA

The tall towers of Aquora were glimmering specks far behind them, as the *Lizard's Revenge* sped through the choppy waters towards Sumara.

"Don't worry," said Lia, standing beside Max on the bridge of Roger's ship. "We'll be back in no time."

Max had said goodbye to his mum and dad at the hospital where Callum was being treated, and he felt a pang at leaving them. His family still hadn't had much time together since Max had rescued his mum after her imprisonment on board the *Pride of Blackheart*.

As if in answer to Max's worries, a voice crackled on the long-range intercom. "Good luck, everyone." It was his mum. "Be careful out there. Those cyrates sound dangerous. Over and out."

"Your mother worries too much," said Lia. "We defeated the Professor and Cora Blackheart. How scary can a bunch of techno pirates be?"

Max didn't reply, but he felt a prickle of unease run down his back. "I'm not sure…those cyrates use tech far beyond the knowledge of any Aquoran – even the Professor." He remembered the cyrate's harsh voice threatening Aquora.

Who is Red Eye? And what does he want?

"Faster, Uncle!" cried Grace. She was standing at her uncle's side, grinning from ear to ear. She'd tied coloured ribbons in her hair, and a tricorn hat was perched jauntily on her head.

Through the bridge window, Max could see Rivet gambolling on deck, barking up at gulls. Ahead, Spike's dorsal fin cut through the water.

I nearly forgot! Max turned to Lia. "I need to show you something. Come with me."

He led her below deck, down several flights of stairs to the cargo bay. There was something waiting there, veiled by a heavy tarpaulin.

"I've been working on this for ages now," Max told her as they dragged the tarpaulin off. "I know tech's not really your thing – but isn't it great?" Underneath the tarpaulin sat a gleaming one-person mini-sub, shaped

like a manta ray. “It’s my own version of the hydrodisk!” Max explained. “It has all the latest weapons, plus it’s the fastest sub under the seas.”

Lia rolled her eyes. “You Breathers and

your technology," she sighed. "Hey, what's going on?"

Max looked up from the hydrodisk to realise that the ship had stopped. The next moment Roger and Grace came climbing down the spiral metal stairs. "We've arrived," said Roger. "Time to take a dip."

With everyone gathered in the cargo bay, Max opened a closet that contained several sizes of deepsuits.

"Grace, you can stay and look after the ship," Max said, taking out a suit and handing it to Roger.

"That's not fair!" Grace cried in outrage. "Uncle? Don't you dare try to leave me behind!'

"Is there a suit small enough for her?" asked Roger. He gave Max a helpless shrug. "I did promise to show Grace some of the wonders of Nemos."

"She'll be safe enough with us," said Lia, picking a small deepsuit and helping Grace into it.

Roger pressed a lever and a wide door ground slowly open, revealing the waves churning and slapping the hull below them.

Lia took Grace's hand and jumped with her into the sea. Meanwhile Max climbed into the hydrodisk and signalled Roger to give it a push along its metal runners. It slid along and curved down into the water.

Max heard a small splash, and turned to see Rivet swimming alongside – he must have jumped from the deck above. Max angled the hydrodisk's nose downward for the long dive to the underwater city of the Merryn.

Grace and Roger powered along under the water on their deepsuits' rocket jet boots, leaving long foaming trails behind them. Lia streaked past the hydrodisk, giving Max a quick wave as Spike swam strongly in her wake.

They soon came to the ocean bed with its towering outcrops of rock and its deep valleys of silt and seaweed.

As they crested a sharp ridge, the astonishing sights of Sumara came into view.

"Wow!" gasped Grace. "Look at that, Uncle!"

Coral spires and steeples shimmered gently in the deep water. As they came closer, they saw the familiar graceful statue that towered over the wide, open central square.

"That's Thallos, our god," Max heard Lia telling Roger and Grace over their headsets. She pointed to an imposing building that dominated the whole city. "That's the Coral Palace, just beyond the Arch of Peace."

"I've never seen the like!" breathed Roger in amazement.

"Who lives in the palace?" asked Grace.

"Lia's father, King Salinus," said Max.

Grace gazed at Lia in wonder. "You're a princess?" she said. "I'd love to be a princess. A pirate princess, of course."

Lia smiled. "Maybe you will be, one day," she said.

They came to rest in the courtyard at the front of the palace and Max climbed from his hydrodisk. The guards recognised him and Lia and waved them through.

They found King Salinus seated upon a throne of pearls, speaking with a group of his advisors.

"It is a joy to see you," he said, smiling and taking Max and Lia by the hands. "And who are your companions?"

"This is Roger, a good friend," said Lia.

"And I'm Grace," piped the little girl through her deep-sea mask. "Princess of all the pirates!"

"Delighted to meet you, your most Royal… er…Fishyking…" mumbled Roger, bowing awkwardly.

King Salinus raised an eyebrow.

"We've come to see Tarla," Lia explained to

her father. "We need her to read something written in ancient Merryn."

King Salinus clapped his hands and two guards appeared. "Summon Tarla the healer at once," he said.

"Your city has treasures that are worth a lot of money, I dare say," said Roger, while they waited for Tarla.

"It is not my city," the king said gently. "It belongs to all my people."

A door opened, and Max smiled as an elderly Merryn lady with long wispy hair and piercing blue eyes came in.

"Tarla, welcome," said the king, showing the old woman to a seat. "We have need of your skills."

Rivet jumped onto the table and Max pressed a button on his snout. A small 3-D hologram of the map appeared.

"This map shows the Chaos Quadrant,"

Tarla said. Her fingers followed the lines of runic letters. "The writing tells of four ancient weapons that are hidden there. The Arms of Addulis!"

"The what of who?" asked Max.

Lia pointed to a painting on the far wall of the throne room. It showed a strong-looking Merryn warrior, his face stern and fearless, his body sheathed in armour.

"That's Addulis," she explained eagerly. "He was the first king of Sumara. He led our people in the war against the humans."

"That was many centuries ago," added King Salinus. "He wielded four objects which could channel the greatest powers of the ocean."

"Four Xs...one for each weapon," said Max.

"Together they made him almost invincible," said Lia. "But after the war ended, the Merryn and the humans drew up a peace

treaty, and King Addulis ordered his chief councillor to hide the weapons in a distant place so their deadly powers could never be used again."

Max eyed the hologram uneasily. "Red Eye must be trying to get his hands on the Arms of Addulis."

"If he does, all of Nemos will be in danger," added Roger.

Max felt a thrill of fear run through his

veins. "And Aquora will be his first target!" He brought his fist down on the table. "We have to stop him!" he declared. "We have to find the Arms of Addulis first!"

CHAPTER FIVE

TERROR AT SEA

Soon they were back on the bridge of the *Lizard's Revenge*, Roger at the helm, guiding the ship over the borders of the Chaos Quadrant. The old pirate glanced at the hologram map projected from Rivet's snout.

The dogbot scratched himself with a metal paw, and the image flickered.

"Still, boy," Max said, soothingly. Looking at the map, he could tell they were close to the first X, which marked the first of the legendary Arms of Addulis.

I just hope Red Eye hasn't got there first. Max looked out over the darkening seas. *He's out there somewhere.*

"I wish your dad could have spared us a few Merryn soldiers," Roger moaned to Lia.

Lia eyed him. "If I didn't know better, I'd say Grace was the braver of you two," she said.

"Not at all!" spluttered Roger. "It's just we need all the help we can get against Red Eye and his cyrates."

"We have a treaty with the Pirate Council of the Chaos Quadrant," replied Lia. "It forbids Sumarans to enter their domain under arms. And in return, they promise not to attack us."

"Tell us more about these Arms of Addulis," Max said to Lia. "Are they really that powerful?"

"More powerful than any tech," she replied. "The first weapon is the Pearl Spear. It channels the strength of the most powerful sea beasts to its wielder. It can pierce the thickest armour with a single blow. Then there is the Stone Breastplate, forged in the depths of the ocean. It can resist any force that comes to bear on it. The third is the Coral Sword. Anyone who wields it will be able to fight with all the speed and agility of the swiftest of fish. And lastly there is the Shell Helmet, from the first ever ocean creature. Anyone wearing it will find their Aqua Powers increased tenfold. They will be able to command sea creatures in their thousands!"

Roger snorted. "Old legends meant to scare little Merryns into eating their seaweed!"

"I don't know," said Max. "Red Eye must think the Arms of Addulis are real. Why else would he steal the map?" A thought troubled him. "But why would someone who commands advanced submarines and cyrates be interested in ancient Merryn weapons?"

"A pirate with all that tech, and the Arms of Addulis as well, would be unstoppable," Lia murmured.

"He'd be the deadliest enemy we've ever fought," agreed Max, as a chill ran down his spine.

"It's dark ahead," said Grace, clearly not listening to the others. She was gazing out over the ocean.

She was right – the seas had darkened to an eerie gloom. Huge black clouds had blown over the ship out of nowhere. The air chilled and wind howled in gusts over the bridge's viewing screen.

"Prepare for stormy weather, shipmates,"

said Roger, gripping the wheel. "We're in the Chaos Quadrant. We'll find no peace here."

The boat began to toss on rising waves; Max had never seen a gale blow in so fast.

"Grace, you'll be much safer if you stand here with me," said Roger, grimly clinging onto the wheel.

"No thanks," cried Grace, hanging onto a rail as she stared excitedly out of the window.

The others braced themselves as best they could. Max saw that Lia's eyes were closed. *She's using her Aqua Powers to check Spike's still with us*, Max realised. They could easily lose the swordfish in a storm.

"I'm deploying the auto-stabilisers," Roger said.

Max was familiar with the technology. Only minutes later, the waves were rising like mountains around them. But the ship remained steady, as if sailing within an invisible forcefield. "The waves are forced to break by jets of current, fired by the stabilisers," Max explained to Lia, who still looked like she would much prefer to be underneath the water.

She glared at him. "Stillfish can do a much better job of calming waves," she replied.

Suddenly the ship lurched and a siren began wailing on the bridge. Cascades of

green seawater broke over the ship's bows and crashed onto its decks.

"The stabilisers have gone," Roger wailed. "And no boat can withstand a Force 12 Chaos gale. We're doomed!"

Out of nowhere, Max saw a huge dark wave rushing in from the port side.

"Watch out!" he cried as the wave slammed into the ship, making it tilt wildly. Max clung

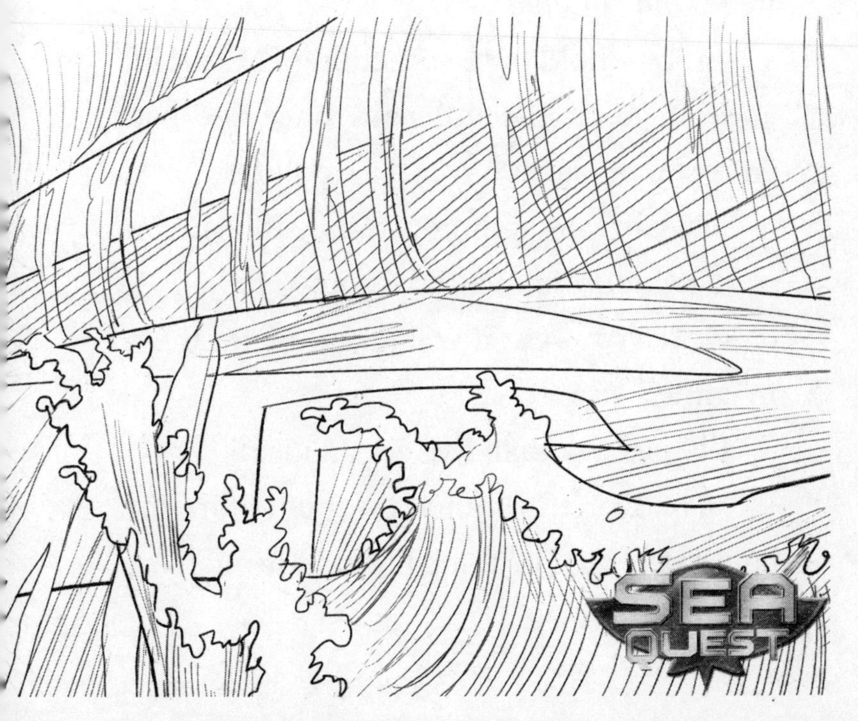

on with one hand, grabbing Grace as she was shaken loose from her perch by the window. He saw Roger and Lia sliding down the dangerously leaning deck.

Then, with a sickening lurch, the ship righted itself, tossing them about like dolls. Max saw the whole ocean writhing and churning before his eyes.

Unless we find a way to fight this storm, we're going to sink!

"Grace – hold onto something," Max said, and let go of the little girl once she had wrapped her arms around a steel post.

"Lia, can you summon those stillfish you were talking about?" Max shouted to her.

"Of course – but it will take time for them to come."

"I'll give you that. I've got an idea."

"Max! Don't!" shouted Lia, but before she could stop him, he flung himself through the door of the bridge.

"Careful, Max!" Rivet barked.

The dogbot's whines were lost in the roaring wind as Max climbed down to the lower deck, lashed by spray. He struggled along to a doorway, the storm almost tearing him from the ship.

He hauled the door open and slammed it closed behind him. Panting, he wiped seawater out of his eyes.

That was hard!

He made his way, half-falling, to the cargo bay.

The ship was rocking violently, but he managed to claw his way to his hydrodisk and grasped the lever to open the exit doors in the hull. *I hope I don't wreck the ship.*

Max pulled the lever. Immediately a great wave washed in through the opening cargo door, almost washing him off his feet. He clung onto the sub, pulling himself up and into the hydrodisk.

The water swirled around the cargo bay, picking up the hydrodisk and dragging it through the doors into the storm.

For a few desperate moments all Max could see was flying spray and rushing water. He started the engine, grabbing hold of the joystick controls, his knuckles white. He rammed them downwards. The hydrodisk struck the sea and knifed under.

Under the waves, the water was a swirling froth...

"Max? Are you all right?" It was Lia's desperate voice over the intercom.

"Yes," he replied. "I'm going to steady the ship."

He gunned the hydrodisk directly under the *Lizard's Revenge*, steering it in a tight circle. Gritting his teeth, he pushed the engine to maximum.

I've got to create enough outward current to stabilise the ship. He felt a heavy pressure on his chest and was driven back into his seat by the sub's acceleration. The hydrodisk roared as it spun around and around, under the ship's hull, catching up with its own wake.

"Is that better?" he asked into the mic.

"I think it's working!" cried Lia.

It was as Max had hoped. The hydrodisk was moving so fast that it was creating an area of calmer water within its speeding circle.

"There's no water coming over the decks now," said Lia. "The stillfish are on their way, too!"

No sooner had she said it than Max saw them: mighty fish leaping in from all sides.

"Nice one, Lia!" Max slowed the hydrodisk, allowing the fish to swim beneath the boat.

Spike swam quickly past, seeming to guide the other fish, showing them where to swim. Once they were there, the hair-like filaments that grew along the sides of their sleek bodies began to move in long ripples, calming the waters.

Roger's voice came through the intercom. "I can steer better now."

Max lost track of time as they pushed on. He helped Spike guide the stillfish to whichever side of the ship was most in need, keeping the vessel balanced. Eventually Max noticed a blue tear in the clouds above the surface. The light began to grow, as the sea settled down.

They had beaten the storm!

"We're in the very heart of the Chaos Quadrant now, Max," Roger told him.

"According to the map, the first of the Xs is dead ahead."

With relief, Max aimed his sub upwards, shooting out of the ocean into the air. He skidded on the surface, sending up towers of spray. Around him the horizon was bright blue in some places, but black with storm clouds in others. Here and there, fork lightning stabbed down.

A storm could blow in at any second, he thought. *No one would want to live here.*

Rivet sprang from the side of the ship and dived into the water.

"Max save us!" he heard the dogbot say over the intercom as Rivet swam towards the hydrodisk.

"Good to see you, Rivet," Max said. But as he peered through the watershield, he spotted something. "What's that in the distance?" he asked into his headset.

"We can't tell from here," Lia replied. "Maybe a low-lying island?"

Max pressed some buttons and the hydrodisk's long-range telescope rose from the dashboard. He pressed his eye to the lens.

The dark shape came suddenly into clear view. Max let out a gasp. "It's one of Red Eye's submarines!"

His heart sank. Red Eye was going to get to the first of the deadly weapons before them. Almost before their Quest had started, their enemy seemed to have won.

Max set his jaw.

Not while I have anything to do with it!

CHAPTER SIX

THE BEAST FROM THE DEEP

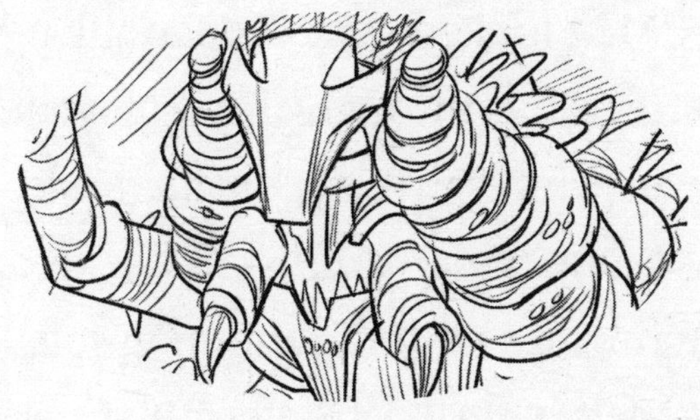

Max spoke into the intercom. "I'm going on ahead. The hydrodisk is much faster than the *Lizard's Revenge* – it's our best chance of getting there before Red Eye."

Grace's voice sounded in his earpiece. "I want to come!"

"No, you'll be safer there on the ship with your Uncle Roger," Max told her.

He engaged the engines and the sleek vessel knifed through the water, closing in on the submarine and the island beyond it. Rivet zipped along at Max's side, his snout lamp glowing red.

"I'm right behind you!" It was Lia's voice. Max looked over his shoulder. Spike was streaming through the water with the Merryn princess riding on his back. They were using the hydrodisk's slipstream to maintain pace with the zooming sub.

Max felt a thrill of determination. *With Lia and Rivet backing me up, things will be much easier*, he thought.

He steered the hydrodisk away from the submarines and into a narrow bay to the side of the island, out of sight.

Max climbed from the hydrodisk, leaping out into the shallows. There was a whoosh as Spike zoomed to a stop. Lia dived from his back and entered the water beside Rivet, who was paddling by the sub.

"Spike will patrol the shoreline," Lia said, as the rest of them headed for the craggy, boulder-strewn shore. Max's heart was racing at the thought of taking on the cyrates again.

This time I'm ready.

They clambered up the rocky shore, keeping low, as a deep vibration shuddered beneath their feet.

What is that?

As they crested a rise, Max saw the skeleton-like cyrates already swarming around a huge drill, moving efficiently like parts of the same machine. Some of them were working on the equipment, others moving the debris away.

Rivet let out a growl when he saw the cyrates and Max patted on him on the head. "Easy, boy."

"What do we do?" Lia murmured as they

watched the cyrates from behind a large boulder.

Max took the cyrate's blaster from his belt and pointed to a tall crag of grey rock that hung over the drilling cyrates. "If I can get closer to that cliff without being seen, I might be able to blast it so it falls down on top of them," he said.

"Rivet help!" declared the dogbot. "Rivet

distract pirates!"

"No, Rivet, stop!" cried Max, but he was too late. The dogbot leaped over the top of the boulder and ran towards the cyrates, barking enthusiastically.

Several cyrates turned their cold red eyes towards the racing dogbot. They drew blaster guns and opened fire.

"Rivet!" Max shouted. "Come back!" But it was too late – they had been spotted. Blaster fire sent splinters of rock flying around them, and they were forced to take cover behind a ridge.

Max peered over the ridge. Rivet was zigzagging, avoiding the blaster rays, barking wildly.

He's trying to help, but he'll be blown to bits!

Luckily the dogbot turned and charged away to a cluster of boulders beyond the drilling sight, dodging the rapid bursts of blaster fire.

Max jumped up, opening fire on the cyrates himself. If he could just keep them busy, maybe Rivet could escape. The blast from his gun sent the head of the nearest cyrate spinning through the air. He aimed again, powering a blast into another cyrate's chest and sending it crashing to the ground in a shower of sparks.

But more kept on coming. No matter how rapidly he fired, they drew closer, and their shots were dangerously accurate. Max could feel the heat of the shots bursting on the rocks by his head. Lia ducked with a cry as a whole section of rock exploded dangerously close to where she was hiding. They broke cover, hurrying closer to the shoreline.

I can't leave Rivet behind, thought Max

desperately, as he ducked behind another mound of rocks. But what else could they do? Unless… Maybe they could take advantage of Rivet's crazy attack. Max handed Lia the blaster.

"Keep shooting," he told her. "I've got a plan. I'm going to make some changes to Rivet's programming."

Lia took the blaster, gripping it awkwardly in her webbed hands. She winced as she pulled the trigger and the first blast burst from the muzzle.

It struck a cyrate in the chest and he fell in a crackling and smoking heap.

"Gotcha!" Lia cried, lining up another cyrate in her sights.

Even if she doesn't trust technology, she's still a good shot, thought Max.

"Keep going!" he shouted.

While Lia blasted away, Max worked

quickly on his wrist device, reversing Rivet's power input.

"Rivet," he ordered, speaking into the headset. "Run towards the cyrates."

"Yes, Max!" came the reply. The dogbot bounded out from cover, straight towards the back of the pacing robots.

Now! Max pressed down on the wrist control.

A powerful electromagnetic pulse erupted from the dogbot, shimmering through the air and making everything in its path waver like reflections in rippling water. When the pulse reached the line of armed cyrates Max was overjoyed to see that his plan worked. The electromagnetic field disrupted the enemies' circuits and stopped them in their tracks. Every one of the cyrates crashed to the ground, their thin limbs twitching.

"Brilliant!" cried Lia, jumping up. They

climbed over the mound of rocks and ran to the drill.

"Rivet do good?" cried the dogbot, his tail spinning in joy.

"Very good," said Max.

The drill had done its work – a great pit had been created in the ground. A metal ladder extended down into it, and right at the bottom Max saw a dark shape among the rubble.

"It must be the chest holding the Pearl Spear," Lia said, in an awestruck voice. "Another few minutes and they would have taken it."

"But now it's ours," Max said, grinning.

Before they could climb down the ladder a loud grinding noise rang out, and Max turned in alarm. A huge hatch was opening in the side of the nearest submarine.

"What's happening?" breathed Lia, her face pale with fear.

"I don't know," said Max, as a wide platform unrolled onto the shingled shore.

A clattering noise echoed from inside the submarine and a grim shape emerged.

"Oh, no," gasped Lia, shrinking back.

Max stared in shock, his blood running cold through his veins.

It was a vast, red-shelled spider crab, covered in pieces of metal and with chainsaws attached to four of its rearing legs. The other four ended in vice-like pincers.

"A Robobeast!" groaned Max as the immense spider crab scuttled down the ramp and came crunching onto the shore towards them. It had a triangular body, horned and crested with metal-sheathed spikes. Vicious claws extended from the wide, snapping mouth and the stalk-like eyes glowed with the same red light as the cyrates.

The creature moved slowly forward on four of its half-metallic legs. The other terrifyingly long limbs waved in the air, the chainsaws buzzing. Stamped into its metal-armoured body was a name: *Sythid*.

"How did Red Eye get his hands on a

Robobeast?" wondered Max out loud. "I thought my uncle was the only person who built them. Even Cora Blackheart had to get him to make them for her."

"Never mind that – we have to get the Pearl Spear before that thing!" yelled Lia, climbing down the ladder. She began to

shovel the rubble away from the chest.

"Quickly!" Max said. Sythid was scuttling over the island towards them, cutting boulders clean in half with its powerful whirling chainsaws.

"I can't open the chest!" Lia cried. "It's still stuck in the rock!"

"I'm coming!" shouted Max. But as he was about to leap in to help her, he heard Rivet's voice.

"Look! Something coming!"

Max saw a tiny one-person repair sub shoot through the waves and beach itself in the shingle. The hatch flipped open and a small figure jumped out.

"I'll get it!" Grace yelled fearlessly, aiming her toy weapon at the creature's hideous face. "Blam, blam."

Max shouted in horror. "Grace! Run!"

But Grace stood her ground, as the Robobeast turned and loomed over her, fixing its pitiless glare on the girl. Its chainsaws whirred faster...

She's going to get herself killed.

Max sprinted towards the little girl, firing at the spider crab as he went. The blasts glanced off the armoured shell and the

Robobeast let out a horrible hissing sound. The chainsaws screamed as they scythed downwards…

CHAPTER SEVEN

CHAINSAWS OF DEATH

Max threw himself forwards, grabbing Grace around the waist and snatching her out of harm's way moments before the chainsaw sliced into the ground, screaming as it gouged through the solid rock.

Holding Grace tightly, Max darted along the beach. He heard the crunch of the creature's legs as it pursued them – moving far more rapidly than Max had expected.

He dived behind a boulder. But two

chainsaws slashed down, grinding through the rock, the noise deafening.

Max flung himself flat with Grace underneath him as shards of stone sprayed them, covering them completely. Sythid's shadow passed over their prostrate forms. *It must think we're crushed.*

"Let go," yelled Grace, squirming in his grip. "I want to fight!"

"Keep still, and keep quiet!" Max hissed.

"Max? Are you all right?" It was Lia's voice, calling from the drill pit.

No! Don't draw attention to yourself! he thought.

But it was too late. The great Robobeast clattered away towards the drill pit. Lia was in danger!

Still holding Grace, Max leaped up, rubble flying off them.

Sythid had reached the pit – but to Max's

relief, he saw that Lia had climbed out and was circling towards him with Rivet at her side. Her face was pale as she watched the Robobeast.

The spider crab towered over the drilling rig, stretching one limb into the pit to feel for the Spear. Max heard it give a frustrated screech.

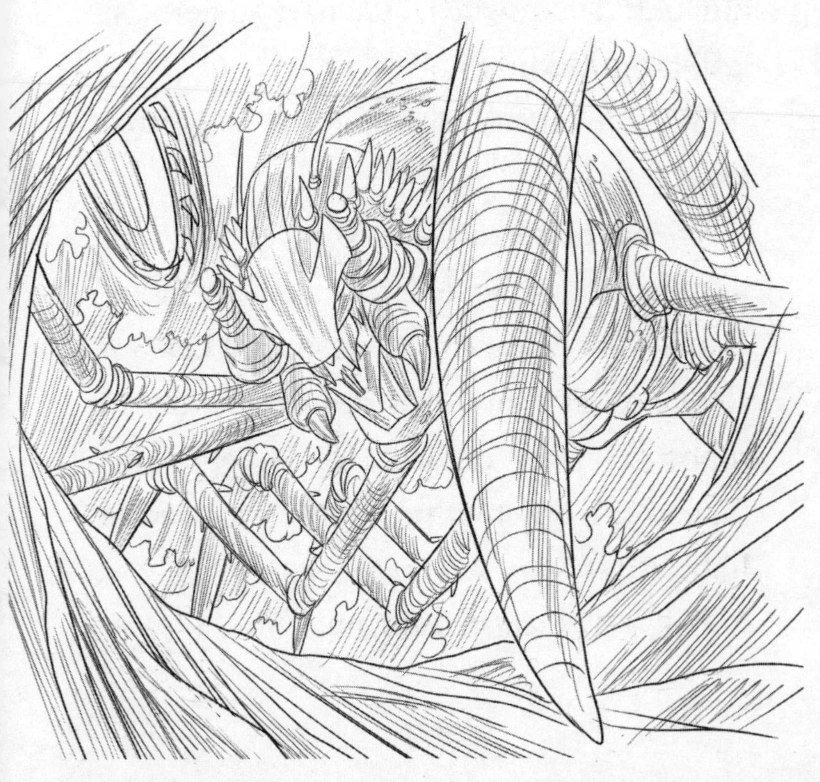

It can't pull the chest loose!

But the Robobeast extended another of its limbs towards the drill, pushing the toothed head back into the hole and starting the machinery again.

"Someone must be controlling it," said Max, as Lia and Rivet reached them. "Someone who knows the Spear needs to be dug out." He frowned. "We have to defeat it fast. If only I knew how!"

"We can attack it head on!" suggested Grace.

"It's too powerful," said Max.

"What about those electromagnetic pulses you used to defeat the cyrates?" said Lia.

"Robobeasts are shielded by hardened robotics," Max replied. He snapped his fingers as a different possibility occurred to him. "Rivet – I need you to scan it."

"Yes, Max!" said the dogbot.

Rivet lifted his head and began to scan the Robobeast while Max watched the results on his wrist control.

"I see something," said Max, freezing a single frame and zooming in on a small unit on the underside of the spider crab's body. "That's the control box," he said. "We need to disable it, so its master won't be able to command it any more."

"It's protected by a metal shield," said Lia. "We'd need to smash that first."

Max stared at the wrist control, wondering how Red Eye could possibly have gained control of the Professor's technology.

"Go, Lia!" Grace's voice pulled Max from his thoughts. He looked up, and was startled to see that Lia had broken cover. She had grabbed his hyperblade and was brandishing it as she ran for the Robobeast.

"No, Lia! You'll be killed!" shouted Max,

scrambling in pursuit. "Grace – keep back!"

Lia had already reached the Robobeast. It seemed unaware of her – the grinding roar of the drill had covered her approach.

But that won't last…

Max's friend ran under Sythid's body, holding the hyperblade in both hands and slashing at the metal plate that protected the control unit.

The blade glanced off the shield.

The crab's swivel eyes stared down at her. One of its limbs lashed out, striking her a vicious blow that sent her sprawling across the beach.

Its eyes burned as it clattered after her.

"Hey! It's me you want!" shouted Max, firing his blaster at the Robobeast. The blasts ricocheted off the spider crab's armour, but he had caught its attention.

"Lia – run!" he yelled. She scrambled to her

feet and flung herself behind a rock. But she had left the hyperblade behind.

Sythid towered over Max, chainsaws roaring. One limb hacked down, but he dived to one side, rolling forwards then springing up again. A second chainsaw slashed, but he ducked, grabbing the hyperblade before

bouncing to his feet.

He swung at the chainsaw, sparks crackling as the vernium blade cut the razor-toothed chain.

Sythid screeched in fury as its chainsaw ground to a halt. But there were still three more. Their chains sped into a blur of screeching teeth, as the beast channelled all its power to its remaining weapons.

It's going to cut me to pieces!

The first chainsaw smashed into the ground by Max's foot. He bounced aside, ducking as the second swung at head height. The third stabbed at his chest, but he pulled back a fraction of a second before it would have ripped through his ribcage. He slashed at the saw, but the Robobeast had learned its lesson. It jerked the chainsaws back out of reach after each blow.

Max was panting now under the relentless

attack of Sythid, striking to right and left as the saws came at him.

I can't last much longer, he thought. *I have to get away!*

But as he backed off the robotic spider crab chased after him, roaring and slashing with its deadly chainsaws.

Suddenly he heard Lia's voice. "The Pearl Spear!" she called.

Max remembered her words back on Roger's boat. *It has the strength of the most powerful sea beasts. It can pierce the thickest armour with a single blow.*

Max gritted his teeth in determination, as he understood. *The Spear will be able to stab through the Robobeast's armour...*

There was still hope. "I'll keep it busy," Max gasped, fighting and dodging for his life. "You get the Spear!"

But could he survive long enough for Lia

to retrieve the weapon?

He saw movement out of the corner of his eye. It was Grace, racing under the spider crab's legs, her toy blaster in her hand. Rivet dashed along behind her.

"Grace bad!" barked Rivet. "Come back!"

Max redoubled his efforts, hacking at Sythid's armoured underbelly – hoping to keep its attention focused on him. To his horror, he saw Grace leap onto one of the spider crab's limbs and crawl up to its body.

What's she doing?!

The blaster fell from her fingers as she jumped onto the Robobeast's shell. "I'll teach you!" she shouted. She crawled forwards and grabbed one of the Robobeast's eyestalks in both hands, wrenching at it with all her strength.

The crab shook itself to try and dislodge her. But she clung on grimly, tugging at the eyestalk, driving the Robobeast wild with fury.

Its chainsaws rose above the little girl, the saws shrieking as they closed in on her.

If he didn't act quickly, Max knew that Grace would pay for her courage with her life!

"Hey! Leave her alone!" Max shouted, springing forwards. "It's me you want!"

One of the Robobeast's chainsaws swung round to the side of him, roaring in his ears.

CHAPTER EIGHT

THE PEARL SPEAR

Max stumbled, falling heavily as the chainsaw cut the air above him. Just before he hit the ground he tucked his legs back, using his momentum to roll to his feet. He jumped over another swiping saw and snatched hold of the spider crab's long, metal-clad limb.

Sythid lifted its leg, trying to shake Max off, but Max leaped upwards, landing surefootedly on top of the creature's shell.

Finding his balance, he ran to Grace, who was still wrenching at the Robobeast's eyestalk. Max heard a shriek behind him and turned, just in time to ward off the blow of a chainsaw with his hyperblade. His arms ached from the effort of the unequal battle.

Sythid swung itself from side to side in a furious effort to dislodge them. Grace's fingers lost their grip and she slid down the curved shell and tumbled to the ground.

Max managed to keep to his feet, relieved to see Grace pick herself up. She was unhurt, but the Robobeast reached for her, chainsaws snarling.

"No!" Max shouted, hacking at the spider crab's shell with his hyperblade. As his blow struck, the creature shuddered and seemed almost to stumble.

Max stared down at the shell. His blade had struck a narrow crevice. Was it some kind of weak spot?

He dropped to his knees and hacked at the crevice again. The spider crab's limbs shook and for a moment, Max thought it might fall over.

"Grace – get away!" Max yelled.

"No! I want to beat that nasty old crab!"

A burst of barking cut her off. "Rivet save Grace!" The dogbot was dragging Grace away from the Robobeast, her deepsuit clamped between his metal teeth.

Good boy, Rivet!

"Lia!" Max yelled, crawling to the front of the shell. "Get the Pearl Spear!"

Lia jumped up and sprinted towards the pit.

The Robobeast's claws twisted upwards, snapping at Max with its cave-like mouth. He knew he could never win this fight, but his attack was keeping the spider crab occupied.

"Got it!" cried Lia, emerging from the pit with an ancient-looking chest, covered with Merryn writing. Max's hair was blown in front of his eyes as Sythid hissed angrily, making for Lia.

Max swung at the Robobeast's snapping

claws with his hyperblade, knowing that at any moment those razor-edged pincers might close on him and bring the fight to a terrible end.

"I have it!" shouted Lia, brandishing the spear. It was as white as bone, dazzling from the reflected rays of the sun. *The Pearl Spear of Addulis!*

"Well done!" shouted Max. "Now we just need to –" Suddenly he lost his balance and slid off the shell. He hit the ground with an agonising thud. One of the Robobeast's pincered legs came lancing down, pinning his hyperblade to the ground.

As he lay gasping and wracked with pain, he saw the chainsaws descending towards him. Max writhed to escape, holding his one free hand up in defence against the colossal crab.

I can't get away this time – this is the end!

"Max – the Spear!" cried Lia, launching the weapon at him.

Max caught the Spear, and felt a strange power running through his arm. He lunged hard, stabbing at the chainsaws.

The Robobeast howled as the Spear sliced into one of the chainsaws. Max winced at the sudden shriek of tortured metal, ducking down as splinters of the broken chainsaw spun through the air.

The Spear gives its wielder the strength of the mightiest sea creatures.

With new heart, Max got to his feet, jabbing the Spear at the Robobeast's limbs.

The spider crab drew back, its red eyes burning with fury, its chainsaws swinging, its claws snapping.

"I can't get near the control unit!" Max shouted in frustration.

"Throw the Spear!" yelled Lia.

Max hesitated. If his aim was off, the Spear would be lost. "It's a Merryn weapon!" he shouted, flinging the Spear to Lia. "You do it!"

The moment that Max threw the Spear,

the spider crab darted forwards. The vice-like pincers of one of its claws caught Max around the waist and lifted him off his feet.

The claw drew him up to its gaping mouth. Tooth-like plates of bone gnashed as Max struggled to get free. The claw clamped tighter, crushing the breath from him. He cried out in pain, his legs kicking, his fists beating at the claw as he was brought closer to that terrible mouth.

He turned his head, seeing Lia leap in under the Robobeast's shell, the Pearl Spear in her hands. She thrust upwards, straight towards the small metal box that must hold Sythid's main circuitry.

Max heard a crackling, fizzing noise. The Robobeast roared, its limbs jerking, the red glow fading from its eyes. The claw loosened around Max's waist and he fell free.

Lia just managed to jump clear as the

spider crab sank to the ground.

She ran up to Max, the Pearl Spear gleaming in her hand. "Are you all right?" she asked.

Max cautiously rose to his feet. "I think so," he gasped, massaging his injured ribs. "It was a close thing, though."

Grace's voice rang out from a little way up the beach, Rivet's teeth still clamped to her sleeve to stop her from joining the battle. "At last. I could have beaten that crab in no time!"

As if in answer to Grace, the creature got up, and all the metal attachments fell away as one. The chainsaws crashed to the ground, and the armour broke apart.

The spider crab turned and scuttled down the beach, going straight for the cyrates' subs. It ripped one open, using its claws like tin openers, revealing a few of the robotic pirates inside. Then it snapped the metal pirates up in its pincers, breaking them into pieces.

"It's getting revenge on the creatures that enslaved it!" said Lia.

Broken and dismembered cyrates were scattered across the beach. The other sub roared to life, zooming off as Sythid chased it, scuttling into the surf.

Grace came racing up as Lia and Max stood on the shore. The little girl was cheering and punching the air. Max smiled wearily at her, too tired from the fight to celebrate.

Out to sea, the giant spider crab turned and looked at them for a moment, lifting its claws as though in a salute.

"It's thanking us," said Lia, raising her hand as the spider crab slipped under the waves.

"Here comes Uncle!" Grace cried as their ship appeared around the edge of the island.

Roger stood at the prow. "Well done!" he called. "Grog all round!"

"I would have helped," Roger explained, when they were all back on the bridge. "But I was afraid those cyrates might take the ship if it was unmanned."

Max didn't say anything, but he noticed Lia rolling her eyes.

"You should have seen me beat that crab!" said Grace. "I did it all on my own!"

Max smiled, not bothering to contradict her. But there was no time to waste – the cyrates still had the map that showed where the rest of the Arms of Addulis had been hidden.

"Where is the next X?" he asked.

"Not far," Roger replied. "I'll plot a course. Don't fret, Roger will lead you true!"

Max stared out over the open sea, thinking hard as the ship powered through the waves towards their next target.

Who was Red Eye? How was he able to create Robobeasts? And why did he want those ancient Merryn weapons?

Max set his jaw. He had no answers to those questions yet, but he knew one thing: with his friends at his side, he would be ready to face whatever was coming.

They were setting out on a new Sea Quest, and while danger threatened Nemos, they would never give up the fight against evil!

Don't miss Max's next Sea Quest adventure,

when he faces

BRUX
THE TUSKED TERROR

COLLECT ALL THE BOOKS
IN SEA QUEST SERIES 5:

THE CHAOS QUADRANT

978 1 40833 471 3

978 1 40833 473 7

978 1 40833 475 1

978 1 40833 477 5

OUT NOW!

Look out for all the books in

Sea Quest Series 6:

MASTER OF AQUORA

FLIKTOR THE DEADLY FROG

TENGAL THE SAVAGE SHARK

KULL THE CAVE CRAWLER

GULAK THE GULPER EEL

Don't miss the

BRAND NEW

Special Bumper Edition:

MONSTER OF THE DEEP

COMING SOON!

WIN AN EXCLUSIVE GOODY BAG

In every Sea Quest book the Sea Quest logo is hidden in one of the pictures. Find the logos in books 17-20, make a note of which pages they appear on and go online to enter the competition at

www.seaquestbooks.co.uk

Each month we will put all of the correct entries into a draw and select one winner to receive a special Sea Quest goody bag.

You can also send your entry on a postcard to:

Sea Quest Competition, Orchard Books,
338 Euston Road, London, NW1 3BH

Don't forget to include your name and address!

GOOD LUCK

Closing Date: 30th April 2015

Competition open to UK and Republic of Ireland residents. No purchase required.
For full terms and conditions please see www.seaquestbooks.co.uk

DON'T MISS THE

BRAND NEW SERIES OF:

Series 15: VELMAL'S REVENGE

978 1 40833 487 4

978 1 40833 489 8

978 1 40833 491 1

978 1 40833 493 5

COMING SOON